P9-CNI-716

Julie Andrews Edwards
and Emma Walton Hamilton

LITTLE BO in LONDON

THE ULTIMATE ADVENTURE OF BONNIE BOADICEA

ILLUSTRATED BY Henry Cole

An Imprint of HarperCollins*Publishers*

Little Bo in London: The Ultimate Adventure of Bonnie Boadicea

For information address HarperCollins Children's Books, a division of HarperCollins Publishers, 10 East 53rd Street, New York, NY 10022.
www.harpercollinschildren.com

Library of Congress Cataloging-in-Publication Data
Edwards, Julie, date
Little Bo in London: the ultimate adventure of Bonnie Boadicea / Julie Andrews Edwards and Emma Walton Hamilton ; illustrated by Henry Cole. — 1st ed.
p. cm. — (The Julie Andrews collection)
Summary: After helping to foil a hijacking on their yacht, Bo the cat, her friend Panache, and owner Billy Bates sail to London for an audience with the Queen.
ISBN 978-0-06-008911-5 (trade bdg.)
[1. Cats—Fiction. 2. Voyages and travels—Fiction. 3. London (England)—Fiction. 4. England—Fiction.] I. Hamilton, Emma Walton. II. Cole, Henry, date, ill. III. Title.
PZ7.E2562Lil 2012 2010013685
[Fic]—dc22 CIP
AC

13 14 15 16 LP 10 9 8 7 6 5 4 3 2

❖

First Edition

For young adventurers everywhere
—J.A.E. and E.W.H.

To S.S.—wise and patient friend
—H.C.

CONTENTS

CHAPTER ONE

Heading for the Islands

THE BEAUTIFUL MOTOR sailer *Legend* sliced through the azure-blue waters of the Mediterranean Sea with grace and speed. Her tall sails were raised and their canvas was taut. It was a sparkling late summer day—perfect for a cruise to the Greek Islands.

On the bridge—the command center of the yacht—the little gray Persian cat, Bo, was stretched out in her favorite spot: by the windshield, on top of the console. The sun was warm on her fur, and she was lazily relaxing, half dozing but nevertheless acutely attuned to every move that her best friend and favorite human in all the world, Billy Bates, was making. The young sailor was at the ship's wheel, piloting the stately vessel, and beside him stood Captain Ian Fraser. The two men shared a companionable silence, the only sounds being the gentle hiss of the sea as it passed beneath the boat's hull and the wind buffeting the sails occasionally and pulling the tightly lashed bindings with a gentle tug. Bo was by now so accustomed to being at sea, after her many travels with Billy, that sailing was as natural to her as breathing, and she loved it.

Bo's eyes opened the tiniest bit, and she saw that Panache—the marmalade cat who had invited himself aboard their cruise—was comfortably curled up on the leather banquette on the other side of the bridge. Bo felt content and very lucky. From the day that Billy had rescued her on a quayside in England, wet and cold and separated from her family, to his taking her aboard the herring boat where he was once employed, to their trip together to Paris and their adventure on a barge heading down to the south of France, to their being asked to come aboard *Legend* to work for its delightful owners, Lord and Lady Goodlad—well, life just kept getting better and better.

Bo vividly remembered the day when she and all her siblings were about to be drowned in the river by the cruel butler, Mr. Withers, and how it was Maximillian, her very smart brother, who had sensed that something terrible was about to happen and urged them all to escape—to "Run! Run as fast as you can in every direction!" They had all done just that.

Bo often thought of her mama and papa, and her lovely sister Princess, the one kitten in the litter left safely at home. If only she could see them again one day and share the news of all the family and her many adventures. It had been such a happy accident to find her brother Tubs in Paris, where he now lived with a kindly chef. Recently *Legend* had been sailing along the coast of Italy, and Bo had seen her third brother, Samson, performing with lions in a circus, and had later found her sad little sister, Polly, lonely, ill and lost in the great Colosseum in Rome. Bo had been able to help her, and now Polly lived with a loving family.

The only sibling yet to be found was Maximillian. Bo had made a vow to keep searching until she found him.

Captain Ian sighed. Placing his arms on the console and gazing out at the blue-green waters, he said, "It's days like this—so utterly perfect—that I shall miss when I retire."

"Oh, sir, I hope retirement's a long way off . . . ," Billy answered.

"Well, I've been considering it. The children, my wife . . . I would like to spend more time with them. I've traveled so much—loved every moment of it—but mostly it was without my family. I miss them."

The ship's cook, Lucy, came up the stairs to the bridge, carrying a tray with mugs of tea and a plate of biscuits.

"Ah! Good timing, Lucy. Thanks!" Captain Ian rubbed his hands and added three heaping teaspoons of sugar to his mug.

"Dinner plans, skipper?" Lucy asked as she handed Billy his tea and set down a saucer of milk for Bo and Panache.

"I'll have a word with His Lordship and let you know soonest," the captain replied.

"And speak of the devil, here I am!" Lord Barnaby Goodlad appeared on the bridge, smiling and carrying his own mug of tea. "I was just thinking, Ian, we should go over plans for the rest of the trip."

"Yes, sir." Captain Ian bent over a large map on the chart table and pointed. "We're here now and should be in the vicinity of Marsala by midnight. We could make a straight run for Crete, if you like—travel all night. It would get the long stretch out of the way."

"My thoughts exactly." His Lordship nodded. "If you take the helm after dinner, Cap'n, then Billy and I will take the midnight watch until four A.M. That'll give you and Wally some rest before the remainder of the journey. And your cabin's close by if we need you. Speaking of which"—Lord Goodlad lowered his voice—"since we'll be in open waters, we'll take the usual precautions. I don't anticipate trouble, and Lord knows *Legend* is better equipped than most, but ever since the recent kidnapping attempt on my beloved wife in the south of France, we can't be too careful. Vigilance is the best defense. We've done the drill many times. No need to speak of this with Jessie around, or Lucy and Marie-Claire for that matter. But make sure the girls double-lock their cabin when they retire. You and Wally should do the same, Billy. I'll see we're locked and safe in our quarters."

"Aye aye, sir."

"Batten down the hatches tonight, do an extra patrol now and then, and maybe keep the deck lights on. Check fire hoses and flares, have the pepper spray handy . . . oh, and keep the carpet tacks and thumbtacks at the ready."

"Carpet tacks and thumbtacks?" Billy asked after Lord Goodlad left the bridge.

"You'd be surprised how useful they can be if someone tries to come aboard." Captain Ian chuckled. "But they won't be necessary."

Billy certainly hoped they wouldn't. Bo was sitting beside him, and he

rubbed her ears thoughtfully. Better she should be safely out of the way if there were any thumbtacks around.

Bo purred and eyed Panache as he got up to stretch. Arching his back, he delicately flicked one paw after another, then sauntered over to Billy to ask for his own bit of attention.

Billy smiled and scratched the marmalade cat's chin. "Yes, yes, old chap. I haven't forgotten you," he said affectionately. "It's good to have you with us, I must say. You're a good sailor, too."

Panache shook his head as Bo tapped him with a velvet paw. He looked up at her and yawned mightily. "*Incroyable!* Would you believe, *mon amie,* that I am hungry again? Why is it that on a boat all one wants to do is sleep and eat?"

Supper was a simple affair. Marie-Claire, the gentle, pretty young stewardess who had captured Billy's heart, set napkins and silverware for the crew on the bridge. Wally, the engineer, came up from his favorite place, the engine room, rubbing his hands clean on an old rag, and Lucy served hot soup and grilled cheese sandwiches for all.

Lord and Lady Goodlad ate on trays in the small lounge behind the bridge, next to Captain Ian's cabin on the top deck. Bo and Panache sat beside them, enjoying a meal of chicken scraps.

The sun went down, illuminating the sky in glorious colors of rose and burnished orange just before dipping into the water on the horizon's edge and being snuffed out altogether.

"Red sky at night, sailor's delight! We'll have great weather tomorrow," Billy said to Bo as they made a tour of the yacht, checking that all was safe and shipshape. Far away, lights from one or two fishing vessels winked and blinked, presumably heading to harbor and safe haven. As Billy walked back to his cabin, the stars were already a sparkling canopy above.

The young sailor paused for a moment to marvel at the peace and beauty around them. He inhaled the balmy air, fragrant with sea salt and a hint of pine from land unseen. "My word, Bo . . . we are *so* lucky. The planets are

playing hide-and-seek tonight. But look! There's Orion, strong and sturdy as ever. Surely paradise is no more perfect than this."

Billy relaxed in his cabin with Bo beside him until midnight, then took his place on the bridge alongside Lord Goodlad. The command center was lit for night sailing in a soft blue light, its array of equipment panels glowing, pinging and humming as each performed its navigational duty. Bo commandeered her usual place on the console and was soon joined by Panache, who was seldom far from her side.

As Lord Goodlad and Billy chatted quietly and swapped sea stories, the two cats sat together gazing out at the starry night and at the moon casting a soft glow across the water. The sea seemed alive—little waves curling and sparkling with phosphorescence, as though a thousand lights were magically dancing on the surface. Bo was mesmerized by the sight and wondered if Papa had ever seen such a wonder. Occasionally a bigger wave washed over the prow of *Legend*, and a fine spray blurred the windshield. Lord Goodlad turned on the big wipers, and they thudded from side to side, clearing the glass.

Panache sighed. "*Ah, chérie, la vie est bonne*—life is good, huh?"

"It is. And it's beautiful." Bo purred contentedly, feeling warm and safe.

"I am glad you persuaded me to come along for this journey!" the ginger cat stated.

Bo's lovely violet eyes widened with surprise. "Excuse me?" she said. "If I recall, you invited yourself—in fact, you stowed away and surprised us all after we had put out to sea."

"I did? Well, phooey, it makes no difference! This is all too pleasant. Though a little quiet for my taste. I'll be glad when we reach land again."

"Panache, you are never satisfied—always looking for action, always bouncing about! Just like my papa, really. Will you ever settle down, I wonder."

"I doubt it. I hope not! Besides, when I'm with you, there are so many possibilities for adventure. Except right now, of course. . . ." Panache yawned. "I think it's time to find my special pillow in the saloon and retire for the night. *Ah! Regarde, ma chère!* A falling star!"

As Bo looked up, Panache took the opportunity to plant a tiny kiss on her nose, then jumped down quickly and disappeared.

At four A.M., just as the ship's clock gently chimed the hour, Captain Ian and Wally returned to the bridge to take over the next shift.

"All quiet?" asked the captain.

"Yes, skipper. Nothing out of the ordinary. We're just off the southern tip of Sicily," Billy informed him.

"There's the Cozzo Spadaro lighthouse." Lord Goodlad pointed. "You can see the blinks and flashes quite clearly."

"Perfect. Exactly where we are meant to be." Captain Ian smiled his approval. "Thank you, milord. Your turn to sleep. See you back here at oh-eight-hundred hours, Billy."

Lord Goodlad said, "I'll take a longer rest in the morning, Ian . . . lie in a bit." He stretched and added, "This has been a pleasant evening. I love being under way in the dark. Well, I'm off. Good night, lads."

CHAPTER TWO

Intruders

BILLY SIGHED AND settled himself comfortably on his bunk. Bo snuggled in beside him. The thick bedcover was cozy, and after the slight dampness of the bridge, it felt good to burrow down into the warmth. Bo stuck her nose into the comforter and was soon fast asleep.

A mere two hours later she was aware of a small thud overhead—a simple sound, but out of place considering the earliness of the hour. Bo's ears twitched, but she was sleepy, so she ignored the noise. Then it happened again: another thud, followed by a scraping sound. Bo opened her eyes and lifted her head, and beside her Billy stirred.

"Whassall that?" he mumbled, and rolled over to settle into a more comfortable position.

Bo heard Wally's footsteps coming down the stairs to the hallway outside the cabin, but instead of entering their quarters, he whispered at the door, "*Billy!*" Then he knocked on the girls' cabin next door and said quietly, "No problem, ladies! Just stay where you are . . . keep the door locked." His voice sounded a little anxious. Bo heard him open the door to the engine room, and the roar of the powerful engines was suddenly louder for a moment. Then Wally went inside and slammed the heavy door behind him, which produced an even bigger thud.

Billy sat up and rubbed his forehead. "Bother!" he said. "Sounds like the engines have slowed. Maybe a mechanical failure. I guess I'm needed to help." As Bo yawned, he added, "You stay here, little one. No reason to disturb *your* sleep. I'll be back in a moment or two." He quickly slipped into his boating shoes and went topside.

Bo curled up once again, but she didn't feel comfortable anymore. She sensed a familiar prickle on the skin of her neck—a sure sign that something was not as it should be. Climbing onto Billy's pillow, she sat gazing wide-eyed through the open door of the cabin.

The corridor was empty, but she could hear the occasional shuffle on the deck above. Someone was talking, though she couldn't tell if it was Captain Ian or Billy. She waited several moments; then, unable to contain her curiosity and the uneasy sensation that was making her tummy turn somersaults, she jumped from the bunk and padded into the hallway. To her amazement, she came face-to-face with Panache, who was approaching stealthily, cautiously. He, too, seemed a little uneasy.

"*Ah, chérie!* I came to find you," he whispered, a strange excitement in his voice. "*Écoute!* Something is not good. I was asleep in the saloon, but I woke when two bodies came over the back of the boat. They were wearing dark, shiny clothes—all wet—and they disappeared down the stairs to the master cabin."

Bo shivered, knowing her premonition had been correct. Something *was* wrong.

"Where did they come from? How did they find us in the middle of the sea?" she asked.

"I don't know . . . but we should go to the captain and try to get his attention."

"And I must find Billy!" Bo cried, and scrambled for the companionway, but Panache quickly stepped in front of her.

"*Non, non, ma petite!* We must be very careful—we must try to be smart. Let us first find out if anything else is happening."

"Something else *is* happening!" Bo declared. "I heard bumps, and something was scraping!"

"All the more reason to be cautious. Follow me, stay close, and try to become invisible."

The two cats crept up the stairs, their velvet paws making no sound. As they rounded the first corner onto the main deck, they were surprised to see another boat alongside *Legend,* smaller in size. A big searchlight on top of it dazzled the cats with its brilliance. They caught a glimpse of a dark figure inside the boat's wheelhouse.

Panache and Bo crouched down, their bellies touching the floor, and inched their way up the next flight of stairs to the bridge. Peering over the top step, they saw Billy standing at the wheel and a stranger standing just behind him. There was no sign of Captain Ian.

Suddenly a second stranger appeared from Captain Ian's cabin. "He'll not bother us. He's tied up and can't do a thing," he said in a voice Bo recognized but couldn't place.

The speaker stepped into the dim light of the computers on the dashboard, allowing the cats a glimpse of his face. Instinctively Bo hissed,

almost giving away their presence. The man was none other than Jack Haggard, one of two men who had been following the Goodlads and *Legend* ever since the beautiful yacht had departed from the south of France—the same two men who had been dining in the little bistro where Lady Goodlad was almost kidnapped; the same two who had suddenly appeared at the circus in Pisa and later in Rome, on the Goodlads' recent visit to Italy.

"I suspected you two were up to no good," Billy was saying. "You'll never get away with this, you know."

"You hush up!" the man behind him said, and Bo knew that it was Fred Pallid, Haggard's partner. "Just get this yacht up to speed again, turn, and head due north."

"I'm not sure I can do that," Billy replied evenly. "There's a slight problem with the engines at the moment."

"Rubbish! You're just saying that. Where's the other guy—the engineer?"

"He's below, checking the problem."

"Tell him to get up here!" Jack Haggard demanded.

"I don't think he'll come topside, sir. He knows you're here. I'm sure the engine-room door is locked."

"Listen, laddie—does he also know there are two more of us belowdecks at the back? You get this boat moving, and if you or anyone else so much as lays a hand on the radio or any other communications device, it'll be the worse for everyone."

Bo looked at Panache, her heart pounding, and he signaled to her to follow him back down the stairs. The two cats retreated to the lower corridor. It was just as well, for footsteps sounded overhead as someone ran to the bridge. They heard a voice speaking excitedly in a language they didn't understand.

Fred Pallid responded in English. "That's locked, too? Get back down there and keep trying! I'll get on the horn to the boss." The footsteps receded the way they had come.

Bo whispered, "Oh, Panache! What's going on? What do they want?"

"I don't know, but I sense this is very bad for Billy and the Goodlads and all our friends on the boat." Panache's tail flicked back and forth.

"Isn't there anything we can do to help?"

Panache's brow furrowed.

"There is perhaps something we can do . . . though I must warn you, *chérie*, that you, too, could be in grave danger."

"Oh, I feel like such a scaredy-cat," Bo confessed.

Panache blinked at her fondly. "But you are a tower of strength, *ma petite*. Remember all the stories you have told me? The day you ran away in the snow and were chased by a vicious dog, but you got away. . . . And the time you nearly fell from a rooftop in Paris, but you hung on. And how you helped save the baby in the runaway pram, and stopped the car that was going to carry Lady Goodlad away!"

Bo nodded, remembering vividly each frightening incident.

"And your adventures with the lions at the circus—you were so brave! Then you learned to swim in the ocean. And there was the moment in the great Colosseum in Rome, when all the cats were threatening us. . . ."

"*You* were brave, too," Bo reminded him gravely. "You fought Titus!"

"Yes. Well. I am asking you now to join me in being brave like that once again. Shall we try? Shall we steal the moment, little Boadicea?"

At the mention of her proper name, Bo suddenly remembered Papa and what he had said to her one night in the garden at home when she was very young. He had given her the name, saying, "Boadicea is a big, bold name that will help you face the world when times are bad. You can draw yourself up and say, 'You don't scare me one bit, because *I'm* Boadicea—the warrior queen!'"

Bo took a deep breath, drew herself up just as Papa had instructed her to do, and nodded firmly.

"That's my girl," Panache said. "*Alors!* Here is what we are going to do. . . ."

And he leaned closer to whisper in her ear.

CHAPTER THREE

The Great Rescue

ON THE BRIDGE, Jack Haggard helped himself to a mug of steaming hot coffee from a flask that was standing on the console.

Fred Pallid was still on his cell phone. He looked across at his partner and mouthed, "The boss says do not damage the yacht—he wants it for himself."

"Hmmm. So we can't break the doors down. No matter. Lord and Lady What's-his-name are not coming out, so we won't have extra bodies to worry about—they can stay where they are until we get to port."

"The boss wants an estimate. How long before we're there?"

Jack Haggard turned to Billy. "Are you turning this thing around as I told you?"

Billy grimaced. "Trying, sir. It's slow going."

"You're faking, I know it. Well, it won't work. One way to settle this, Fred. Tell the pilot from the other boat to come up here. He'll know how to get this tub moving."

Fred looked a little queasy. "And who will run *his* boat?" he asked.

"Dummy—*you* will! Just do it!"

"But I'm not a sailor—I don't know how to make a boat go."

"You just wiggle the wheel from side to side. Same as a car. Anyway, we don't even *need* the other boat at this point. We can pick you up later." Fred gulped and looked crestfallen. *"Go on!"* Haggard yelled at him.

But before Pallid could move, Bo appeared on the bridge. Deliberately brushing past Pallid's legs, she leaped quickly onto the console.

Jack Haggard smiled for the first time and crossed to her. "Hey! Here's my kitty-cat!" he exclaimed, then muttered under his breath, "Least you *will* be my kitty-cat when this is over. . . ."

He reached for Bo—and suddenly there was mayhem.

Bo avoided his grasp and ducked under his arm—the one holding the coffee mug. She bumped his elbow, and the scalding coffee splashed all

over him. Haggard sucked in his breath with pain, and at the same moment Panache streaked onto the bridge—clawing his way up the trousers and jacket of Fred Pallid and yowling like a wounded hyena.

Pallid spun around in fright, trying to rid himself of the offending intruder. Billy seized the chance he had been waiting for—praying for—and grabbed the small fire extinguisher mounted on the siding of the bridge. He clobbered Haggard on the shoulder with it as hard as he could, then pulled out the pin and doused him with foam. Haggard dropped to his knees. Grabbing the pepper spray, Billy fired it at Pallid just as Panache leaped free of the man's shoulder. Pallid howled, rubbing his eyes in pain.

"Follow me, Bo!" Panache cried.

The two cats streaked around and around the bridge, scattering maps and papers and creating as much diversion as possible. They jumped from console to table to banquette, Bo emitting huge sneezes as remnants of pepper spray tickled her nose. Billy dashed for Captain Ian's cabin to free him as the cats continued to harass the two thugs—dashing between their legs, tripping them up, clawing and scratching them every chance they got.

Haggard caught Bo and tried to contain her with his large, rough hands until she felt she could not draw breath and her bones might break. She cried out in protest, and seeing her distress, Panache jumped onto the man's head and bit his nose—hard. Haggard dropped Bo and shrieked, just as Billy was coming out of the cabin with Captain Ian.

The captain delivered a swift punch to Pallid's chin, and he went down—

out for the count. Billy bound Haggard's hands with the same rope that had been used to tie up Captain Ian.

"Billy—send up a flare!" the captain ordered. "I'll get the fire hose and deal with the other boat."

Billy grabbed the flare gun, heaved open the door of the bridge, and sent a rocketlike object hurtling into the sky. It exploded way overhead, lighting up the misty morning with its powerful glow.

As Captain Ian blasted the little boat alongside *Legend* with a fierce jet of water, Bo heard footsteps running toward them. One of the men Panache had seen earlier at the rear of the boat burst onto the bridge, ready to help his accomplices if needed.

Bo and Panache looked at each other.

"One more time, *chérie?*" Panache grinned wickedly.

As one, they leaped upon him. Bo knocked

over a small box from the console, tipping its contents onto the floor of the bridge. Carpet tacks and thumbtacks scattered everywhere, and the young thug—who had no shoes on—began to dance about, yelping and yipping as the sharp points dug into his feet and the cats' claws ripped at his shoulders. Billy had very little trouble containing him.

The smaller boat suddenly peeled away and roared off across the sea, and Captain Ian returned to the bridge. He and Billy made sure that all three intruders were securely bound and would cause no more trouble. Noticing the cell phone that Fred Pallid had been using, Captain Ian picked it up and slipped it into his pocket. Then, using *Legend*'s internal intercom, he gave Wally, still in the engine room, the all clear and told him to get up to the bridge.

But there was one last hijacker to deal with—the one at the door of Lord and Lady Goodlad's cabin, who was attempting to pick the lock.

At the sight of Captain Ian and Billy approaching, he stopped what he was doing and slowly raised his hands above his head. The captain called out, "We're here, milord—the yacht is secure. The problem is over."

Lord Goodlad unlocked the stateroom door and came out to help tie up the young man, saying, "Great work, lads."

"I'll take this guy up to the bridge, where the other three are being held," Captain Ian declared. "And I'll get on the radio right away."

"No need," Lord Goodlad smiled. "I've been busy, too, you know." He winked at Billy. "I told you this yacht was better equipped than most. I have a second radio hidden in our cabin here. I got through to my office back in London. They'd already received the pirates' demands and alerted the authorities."

"Nasty business all round, sir. I hope it didn't distress milady too much. . . ."

"Fortunately, we were together. I was able assure her that we had planned for just such an eventuality, and that the crew would know what to do," Lord Goodlad said. "Help should be along any moment now. There is a British destroyer in the area—it will be joining us, and we're going to be inundated with the press soon, I imagine. Let's make sure Marie-Claire and Lucy are all right. We'll meet on the bridge in five minutes. I'm eager to hear how you fellows managed this."

On the bridge, Bo and Panache sat side by side, gazing wide-eyed at the four bound and helpless pirates on the floor in front of them.

Panache tilted his head. "They don't look so scary now," he commented.

Bo said, "I *don't* like them being on our boat. I'm glad it's over. . . ."

"You were magnificent, *ma petite*. Are you all right?"

"Yes. You were so strong and brave, Panache. Thank you for helping me."

"*De rien*." He washed his paw nonchalantly. "Another adventure, eh? Ha! *J'adore* the action!"

"I could have done without it." Bo shuddered.

He looked at her affectionately. "I'm glad you were not hurt."

CHAPTER FOUR

All Is Revealed

LORD GOODLAD DECIDED that the safest and wisest thing to do under the circumstances was to cancel the remainder of the vacation and head home to England. Malta was the nearest island with an airport, and there were good berthing facilities in the harbor of Valletta, so *Legend* reversed course and within the hour was being escorted toward the island nation by a flotilla of boats, which included the British naval destroyer, a coast guard cutter, and a handful of assorted yachts and power boats that had picked up Lord Goodlad's signal on the radio or seen the ship's flare and had come to see if they could help.

Helicopters dotted the sky. Some were the escort, some were press. They swooped and buzzed overhead and annoyed *Legend*'s passengers no end. Lord Goodlad was on the phone to his office in London, where hundreds of calls were flooding the lines. Captain Ian was busy dealing with radio communications and still more calls from the British government and the International Criminal Police organization, all the while maintaining contact among the various vessels. A message was sent out that a press conference would be held the minute the Goodlads arrived in port.

The four hijackers were transferred onto the destroyer and into British custody, and it was a good two or three hours before the entire crew and Lord and Lady Goodlad were able to gather for a belated breakfast in the lounge behind the bridge, supplied by Lucy and Marie-Claire, who were only too happy to make their own contribution and restore everyone's sense of well-being.

Bo and Panache were still jittery from the recent turn of events, and the *whumping* of the helicopters overhead along with the air horns and whistles from the boats surrounding them only made matters worse—but they calmed a little with a good meal in their bellies and a lot of tender care from Lady Goodlad, Billy, and the others.

"You mean to say that it was actually the *cats* who first came to our rescue?" Lady Goodlad said with amazement as she stroked Panache on her lap.

"I *am* saying that, milady—," Billy replied.

Lord Goodlad interrupted. "Look. Start at the beginning. How did the thugs get aboard in the first place?"

"We were aware from the radar that a small boat was approaching, sir. This was about oh-six-hundred hours," Captain Ian replied. "They claimed to be the Italian Coast Guard. I must say, they followed every appropriate procedure—repeating themselves three times on the international calling and distress channel, asking permission to board, saying there was an alert in the area for pirates and they wished to do a routine check of our papers. I took the precaution of sending Wally down to protect the engine room as we had always planned, milord, and the vessel

pulled alongside us and two men came aboard."

Billy took up the story. "Wally roused me on his way down to the engine room, sir, and told the ladies to stay put—but by the time I reached the bridge, the intruders had already tied up the skipper and locked him in his cabin. I didn't recognize them at first, but as soon as they spoke, I realized it was those guys who had been following us for so long, Haggard and Pallid. They obviously had little knowledge of boats, for they demanded that I take the wheel and follow their orders. They also informed me that two other armed men were belowdecks."

"Trying to gain access to *our* cabin," Lord Goodlad added grimly.

"I'm so glad Barney was with me." Lady Goodlad looked pale. "I don't know what I would have done otherwise."

His Lordship took his wife's hand. "Go on, Billy," he encouraged.

"They wouldn't let me use communication devices," Billy continued, "so I stalled and pretended there was a problem with the engines, hoping to buy some time and find a way to outwit them."

"And was that when Bo and Panache came to the rescue?" Lady Goodlad asked.

"Indeed they did, ma'am. They burst onto the scene and caused such a perfect distraction, one might have thought they knew what was going on and did it deliberately. I was able to overcome Haggard and Pallid and then free Captain Ian."

"It was still pretty dicey at that point," the captain interjected. "One of the other thugs from below suddenly appeared—and if Bo hadn't knocked the thumbtacks onto the floor, who knows what might have happened."

Lord Goodlad looked at Bo sitting on Billy's lap. "Well, little one," he said finally. "It seems we owe you and your ginger friend a great debt of gratitude." He turned to his wife. "Jessie, I shall never again complain about your love of cats."

"May we know, sir, what the intruders actually wanted?" Lucy asked politely.

"Ah. Of course." Lord Goodlad wiped his mouth with his napkin. "Three things: First, a great deal of money. Second, they wanted the yacht—which they would have undoubtedly reconditioned and used for their own piracy purposes. We have so much sophisticated equipment they would love to get their hands on. Third, and most important, they wanted me to shut down an aspect of my business. I'm not sure if you are all aware that in addition to Neptune Shipping and Steel, I also run a tip-top maritime antipiracy firm. We train security teams and place them aboard vulnerable merchant ships in high-risk areas. These chaps are the best in the world—very Double-Oh-Seven, if you get my drift—and we've been so successful that we've made a considerable dent in the modern-day pirating business."

"Perhaps we should add a pair of cats to each security team from now on," Lady Goodlad quipped, and everyone chuckled.

"The only thing we still have to clarify," Lord Goodlad added, "is which *particular* group these thugs are working for. Who is the mastermind, and where is their base?"

"I think that will be resolved quickly enough, milord," Captain Ian responded. "I retrieved their cell phone and informed the Interpol fellows an hour ago. They'll be able to trace the hijackers' calls."

"Good man." Lord Goodlad nodded approvingly. "Actually, when all is said and done, this was a pretty amateur effort."

"*Ouf!* This was professional enough for me!" Marie-Claire waved a hand as if fending off a swarm of mosquitoes. "My heart is still leaping in my ears!"

Billy said thoughtfully, "We were right in thinking that Haggard and Pallid were up to no good, sir. They must have been in on that original kidnapping attempt on Her Ladyship in France, and when it failed, they redoubled their efforts. As we now realize, they've been following us ever since, looking for the next available opportunity to carry out their plans."

Lord Goodlad nodded. "I think you're absolutely right, Billy." He pursed his lips. "Well, now we must prepare for one last assault, my friends—the press. It's going to be madness once we reach port. No one comes aboard, of course—except security and the harbormaster. We'll handle the press on shore."

WELCOME!
234

CHAPTER FIVE

The Press Conference

FOUR HOURS LATER, the island of Malta came into view, and, escorted by even more boats and small tugs that had sailed out to greet them, *Legend* slowly made her way into the beautiful Grand Harbor of the capital, Valletta. Horns tooted, streamers were thrown, and fountains of water spewed from a couple of the tugs. Overhead, an airplane dragged a banner with a big WELCOME! sign on it, and the British destroyer whooped loudly, sending a startled Bo under a chair for a moment as it, too, came in to anchor and to deliver the four pirate hijackers into the hands of the police.

"It's like a party—a holiday—out there," Billy observed. "How did news get out so quickly? How is it possible that everyone knows about us already?"

Captain Ian smiled. "Modern technology, Billy. The Goodlads have a high profile in England and are well regarded. His Lordship is such a vital part of government there. It's no wonder our hijacking incident has been picked up and broadcast—probably around the world by now. It'll be a three-ring circus for a while. So brace yourself, lad. You and Wally go and prepare to tie us off. I'll get on the bullhorn as soon as I've shut down the engines. Don't say anything to *anyone*."

But the captain's orders proved hard to follow. Every available space on the quay had been taken over by members of the press. Small canopies had been set up to keep the sun off cameras and newscasters. There were TV vans with satellite dishes on top of them and cables strewn everywhere. A mass of photographers jostled one another for the best vantage point. Flashbulbs exploded and newsmen began yelling questions even before *Legend* maneuvered into the berth that had been assigned to her.

The moment Billy and Wally jumped onto the dock to secure the lines, the press surged through the barricades that were holding them back and crowded around the lads, pushing cameras into their faces and begging for information. Policemen rushed in to control them, and Captain Ian addressed the crowd with a bullhorn from the open door of the bridge.

"Please be patient, everyone! The press conference will commence in half an hour. Meanwhile, we ask you to respect the yacht. Keep your distance and allow us to tie up safely. We don't want anyone getting hurt."

The harbormaster came aboard to speak with Lord and Lady Goodlad. Three shiny black limousines bearing diplomatic flags and accompanied by police escorts pulled up. The president of Malta and his prime minister, plus the British high commissioner and her deputy, stepped out, and a pathway was made through the crowd to allow them to board *Legend* also.

Lucy and Marie-Claire bustled about in their white uniforms with the yacht's logo emblazoned near the lapel, serving finger sandwiches, soft drinks, and tea to the distinguished guests. The conversation was all about the recent adventure at sea and how Billy had outwitted the pirates with the amazing help of the two cats. Bo and Panache, curious to see the guests and hopeful of receiving a tasty morsel or two, peeked into the saloon and were immediately scooped up by a proud Lady Goodlad and presented for all to admire.

Half an hour later, the Goodlads, accompanied by Captain Ian and the British high commissioner, walked down the gangplank to a small dais where microphones had been set up for them to address the eager press.

The high commissioner announced that Lord Goodlad would say a few words, after which he and his wife would be prepared to take questions. Lord Goodlad stepped forward, and amid a barrage of flashes and the noise of clicking cameras, he read a hastily prepared statement summarizing the series of events. The moment he finished, the questions came rapidly.

"We understand they were masquerading as coast guard—is that true?"

"Milord! Where were *you* when the hijackers came aboard?"

"Over here, milord! We hear they were tracking your movements for weeks—what were their demands?"

"Milady! This way! How did all this make you feel?"

"Is it true you have two cats aboard who were involved in the rescue?"

Lord Goodlad held up a hand. "One at a time, please. The cats in question belong to a young member of our crew who showed great presence of mind and courage. With the help of the two cats, he managed to overwhelm the intruders, release our captain, and thereby save the day."

There was a stunned silence for a moment, and then the questions came again.

"What exactly did the cats do?"

"May we see them?"

"Who is the young man?"

"What is his name?"

"Where does he come from?"

"Why don't we let the young man speak for himself," said Lord Goodlad.

Billy was sent for, and he came down the gangplank with Bo under one arm and Panache under the other. The press went crazy, snapping photos, zooming in on the cats, shouting out still more questions and begging for just one more picture.

"This way, sir!"

"Over here, young man!"

"To your left!"

“To the right, please!”

“A big smile, now!”

Bo buried her head in Billy’s neck. Panache murmured, *“Zut!”* and ducked

under Billy's arm in an attempt to avoid the blinding flashes.

"Could you turn the cats around, please? We need to see their faces!"

The conference lasted well over an hour and came to a stop only when the high commissioner took the microphone again. "That's it for now, everybody. Thank you! The Goodlads will be returning to England tomorrow, at which point I'm sure a follow-up report will be issued."

But the press seemed undeterred and continued milling around the yacht, attempting to peer into portholes and get shots of her interior, or statements from the other members of the crew, in spite of the local police who remained posted on the dock in an attempt to contain them.

The Goodlads lowered the blinds in the main saloon and in the dining room, where they gathered with the crew and the two cats for supper and a discussion of future plans.

"It's a little like living in a fishbowl . . . ," Lord Goodlad commented. He raised his wineglass for a toast. "Okay, everyone. We're here, we're safe, and it's a blessing. I thank you all for your great courage, and I'm so proud of you. We've been through a very rough patch, but the bad guys have been put away, and I've just been informed that their leader has already been apprehended."

"Special mention to our cats," Lady Goodlad chimed in. "And to *you*, Billy. Ever since we met you in that café where I was almost kidnapped, it seems you have been a lucky charm to us."

Billy felt a glow of happiness. "Thank you, milady. I'm glad to have been of help. And I've often felt that Bo has been the same for me—I've always said that she is *my* lucky mascot. And it's uncanny, really, how much has changed for me since I found her." Billy smiled across the table at Marie-Claire.

"Jessie and I are flying to London tomorrow at four P.M.," Lord Goodlad continued. "I hate to say good-bye to you all, but why don't you rest up here for a few days, then head back to the south of France and put *Legend* in good order. We will look forward to seeing you there on our next break."

Lucy brought in dessert for everyone and announced, "No need to help with the dishes tonight, lads! You run on to bed. You must be exhausted."

Wally grinned and said, "I know I'll sleep like a log—and I didn't do all that much!"

"Rubbish!" Captain Ian chimed in. "You would have disabled the engines for us if necessary. You were just waiting for our signal. Everyone did their part."

Lord Goodlad summed it up. "We'll *all* sleep more easily tonight. I know my Jessie will." He reached across the table to touch her cheek. "Eh, my darling? Nothing more to worry about now. It's all over."

In spite of Lord Goodlad's words, Billy felt he would *never* be able to sleep. He lay on his bunk, stroking Bo, and looked enviously across at Wally, who was already snoring gently in the bunk opposite. Panache was lying at Wally's feet, uncharacteristically preferring to be with company this night rather than sleeping alone in the saloon or on the top deck. His golden eyes were fixed on Bo.

"Oh, little one," Billy whispered. "What a long day. Such an unbelievable adventure . . . and you did *so* much to help." Bo blinked at him—and blinked again. Billy suddenly chuckled. "You're having a hard time focusing, aren't you? Me, too. Those flashbulbs this afternoon were just blinding. Tell you what, Bo: it's possible that by tomorrow you and your friend here will be the most talked-about cats in the whole world."

But Bo wasn't really listening. She felt thoroughly relieved to be safe with Billy, and to know that the horrible ordeal was over. She inched her way up the covers and buried her nose in his neck.

CAT-ASTROPHE AT SEA!

CHAPTER SIX

The Invitation

THE FOLLOWING MORNING Bo woke late. There was no sign of Billy, Wally, or Panache, so she padded upstairs. The Goodlads were in the dining room perusing the international newspapers, which were spread out all over the big table.

"Here's our little celebrity!" said Lady Goodlad. She scooped Bo into her lap, and the cat found herself face-to-face with her own image. On the cover of every newspaper were photographs of Bo, Billy, Panache, the captain, and the Goodlads, with headlines trumpeting:

"CAT-ASTROPHE AT SEA!"

"HAIR-RAISING HIJACKING—WONDER CATS RESCUE SHIPPING MAGNATE!"

"*DES CHATS COURAGEUX!*"

"CATS CATCH CRAFTY CROOKS!"

"*I GATTI SALVANO IL GIORNO!*"

"FANTASTIC FELINES FOIL FELONS!"

Captain Ian tapped on the dining-room door. "Morning, sir. Just thought you might want to know that it's the top story on every news channel . . . the television is on in the saloon, if you'd care to take a look."

Lord Goodlad pushed his chair back from the table. "Must be a slow news day." He chuckled. "Let's *all* have a look." Taking his mug of coffee with him, he led the way into the main saloon. Bo and Panache followed, curious to see what all the fuss was about. The hijacking incident seemed to be the only news that mattered.

Gazing at the footage from the press conference, Lord Goodlad said to his wife, "You look very fetching, darling."

She smiled and replied, "Aren't the cats *adorable*?"

The Goodlads began to pack in preparation for their departure, but at midday they received a surprise visitor. The deputy high commissioner had returned to the dock and was requesting permission to come aboard. She ascended the gangplank, a trifle flushed and breathless with excitement.

"So sorry to bother you again, milord," she said as she removed her high-heeled shoes and padded into the saloon. "But I have some rather important news. Our press office has just received a fax from Buckingham Palace—er, by the way, how are you today?"

A little smile played around the corner of Lord Goodlad's lips. "We are all just *fine*, thank you," he said.

"Good, good. Well!" She took a deep breath. "It seems that Her Majesty was dreadfully concerned to hear of your ordeal. She wishes to extend an invitation to you and Lady Goodlad to visit with her at your earliest convenience. She would also like to acknowledge the young man—Billy, is it?—who played such a major role in your rescue."

The Goodlads looked surprised.

"Well! How very kind of her," said Lady Goodlad.

"She's always been a good egg," Lord Goodlad said with a smile. "It will be grand to see her again."

The deputy high commissioner nodded. "Yes! There's just one more thing. She'd very much like to meet the cats. . . ."

His Lordship roared with laughter. Lady Goodlad clapped her hands. "Oh, that's delightful! Barney, do you think it's possible?" she said.

Putting an arm around his wife's shoulders, he said to the deputy high commissioner, "Please convey to Her Majesty that we would be honored to pay her a visit . . . cats and all."

* * *

Lord Goodlad summoned the crew.

"Change of plan, chaps," he said. "We've had a request from Her Majesty to bring Billy and the cats to Buckingham Palace. Billy, it seems you're quite the man of the hour!"

Billy's jaw dropped, and he sat down rather suddenly. It was just as well, for Captain Ian thumped him on the back, and Marie-Claire and Lucy hugged him with delight. Wally gave him a big high five.

Lord Goodlad continued. "Jessie and I have been chatting, and I think the best thing is for us to fly out this afternoon as planned, and for you all to sail the yacht up to London. This way the cats can make the journey with the least amount of upheaval, and they'll stay in their familiar environment. I presume they've had their microchipping, shots, blood tests, and so forth?"

Billy found his voice. "All their papers are in order, milord."

"Perfect. We'll meet up in London in two or three weeks. Not to worry, ladies. It'll be a safe route back."

Captain Ian drove the Goodlads to the airport. They were followed by members of the press who were still hanging around, hoping for more gossip to print. The reporters trailed Captain Ian back to the boat, where they harassed him for information and one more photo of the cats. The captain refused and said to Billy, "It's still a bit of a circus out there. Let's top the boat up and then, for heaven's sake, let's get back to sea as quickly as possible."

And so it was that *Legend* and her crew set sail on a bright morning three days later and headed for England. Over the next two weeks, they crossed the Mediterranean, passing between Sicily and Africa, heading along the Spanish coast and through the Strait of Gibraltar, then beating up the coast of Portugal into the windy Bay of Biscay, to finally round the western elbow of France and enter the English Channel. They navigated the Strait of Dover between England and France and eventually eased their way into the great Thames Estuary, to cruise comfortably toward London.

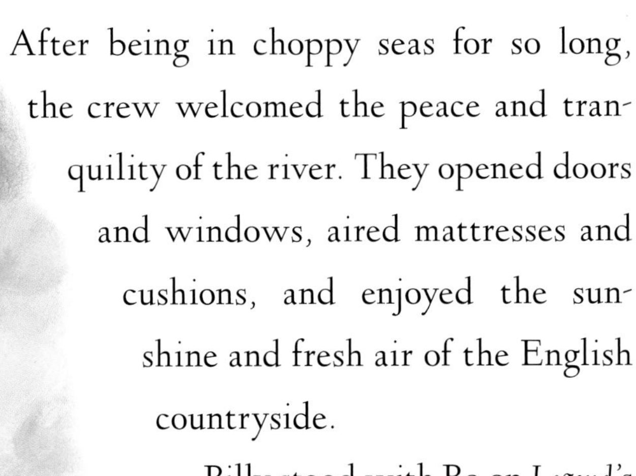

After being in choppy seas for so long, the crew welcomed the peace and tranquility of the river. They opened doors and windows, aired mattresses and cushions, and enjoyed the sunshine and fresh air of the English countryside.

Billy stood with Bo on *Legend*'s prow, waving to curious children who were running along the river path admiring the beautiful yacht.

"We're home, Bo," he said. "Who'd have thought we'd be returning under these circumstances?" He set her gently on the deck. The soft breeze ruffled her fur, and her nose twitched as she inhaled the scents of the river. Panache, never far from her side, joined her.

"This is where I come from, Panache," Bo said, a little wistfully. "Oh, if only I could catch a glimpse of Mama, Papa, or Princess!"

"Where would they be, *chérie*?" he asked kindly.

"A long way from here, I think." She sighed.

The countryside soon gave way to more urban scenery: cargo docks, factories, waterfront industries. Barges, tankers, and other craft navigated the river. Homes, lighthouses, and churches dotted the landscape, dominated by taller high-rise office and apartment buildings behind them.

Lord Goodlad had arranged a berth for *Legend* in the shadow of the famous Tower Bridge. It was a spectacular edifice—two granite towers, each like a tall, thin castle topped with gilded turrets, seemed to grow up out of the center of the river. Near the top, a sky-blue, lattice-trimmed walkway supported and connected them, and below that the main bridge itself allowed cars and buses to cross from one side of the river to the other.

As *Legend* approached her mooring, Bo was astonished to see the lower bridge suddenly split open and its two halves rise up on either side to allow a large navy ship to glide through.

Just as the crew began to secure *Legend* to the wharf, the captain called down from the bridge. "Look out, Billy! We've got a welcoming committee. . . ."

Reporters were running toward them, cameras flashing.

"When are you heading to the palace, Billy?"

"Where is Bo?"

"Can we get a photo?"

Billy scooped Bo into his arms and ducked inside, shutting the doors quickly.

"Some welcome!" he said to Marie-Claire, who was straightening and dusting the main saloon and restoring items that had been stowed for the long journey.

She smiled at him impishly. "Well, now you are a celebri-tee, you must bear and grin at it, I think!" Billy sputtered with laughter.

The Goodlads came to welcome their crew to London. It was a happy reunion, and Captain Ian shared details of the ship's log and their recent journey. Lucy served tea and cookies for everyone. Lord Goodlad said, "We're expected at the palace tomorrow, Billy, at four P.M. We'll come and fetch you and the cats." He chuckled. "It should be an interesting afternoon."

Lady Goodlad petted Bo and Panache. "Hello, my lovely ones! You seem none the worse for wear after your long journey! Look what I brought you. . . ."

She produced two exquisite leather collars. Bo's was silver, decorated with small rhinestones. She gave Panache a copper-colored one, ringed with gold studs. Dangling from each collar was a small medallion with the cat's name and a phone number engraved upon it.

As she fastened them around the cats' necks, Panache glowered at Bo, his ears flattened to his head.

"*Zut alors!* Who does she think I am? Puss in Boots?" he hissed.

Bo squinted at him. "Actually, I think you look very dashing," she said.

"Well, I want it off as soon as possible!" Panache grumbled. "I am not one to be tied down. I am a free spirit!"

But the collars were only the beginning of the insults Panache had to endure, for the following morning both cats were shampooed, brushed, spritzed, and manicured in preparation for their royal visit.

"This better be worth it!" Panache growled sulkily, but he couldn't resist taking a sideways peek at himself in the mirror.

At three o'clock, Billy poked his head out of his cabin.

"Does anyone know how to tie a tie?" he called sheepishly. "I can only do nautical knots. . . ."

"*Certainement!*" Marie-Claire replied, and in a matter of seconds she had fixed him up appropriately and helped him into his jacket.

Bo blinked, for this was a Billy she had never seen. He was attired in the yacht's formal uniform—black shoes, navy trousers, crisp white shirt, black tie, and a handsome double-breasted blazer with gold buttons and gold stripes on the cuffs of the sleeves.

Marie-Claire placed a white cap with a black brim and gold braiding squarely on his head and then tipped it rakishly to one side. She took a step back and surveyed him for a moment.

"Am I presentable?" he asked shyly.

"*More* than that," she said lovingly. "Good luck, Billee." She placed a gentle kiss on his nose.

Wally came out of the engine room, his ever-present oily rag in hand. "Blimey!" he said in surprise. "Who's the new crew member?"

Lucy whistled admiringly, and as they moved upstairs to prepare for departure, Captain Ian commented, “Very nice, Billy. Remember that you represent the yacht and all who sail on her.”

13

CHAPTER SEVEN

Buckingham Palace

THE GOODLADS ARRIVED at the dock in a chauffeured limousine, and just before three fifteen they and Billy and the two cats departed for the palace. Everyone aboard *Legend* cheered and waved as the car drove away. The limo crossed the Tower Bridge and passed along the Victoria Embankment beside the river.

London looked like a wonderful watercolor painting, everything bathed in a soft light—clean and white and pretty. Sitting on Billy's lap and looking out the window, Bo saw big, red double-decker buses, taxis, and pedestrians everywhere. A mighty Ferris wheel was on the opposite side of the river, spinning slowly, carrying sightseers up and over for a spectacular view across the city. The Houses of Parliament—gilded and turreted—loomed into view, and Big Ben rang the half hour sonorously just as they passed it, making Bo twitch with alarm.

Lord Goodlad said to Billy, "There's a lantern in the small tower on top of that great clock. When Parliament is in session long into the night, the lamp is switched on so the public can see that its government is working late."

"Do you go in to work most days, sir?" Billy asked.

"Not every day, no. But I do have an office there, as well as the one at the shipyards, of course."

Lady Goodlad smiled, stroking Panache, who was lying beside her. "Nervous, Billy?" she inquired.

Billy thought about it. "Not exactly nervous, milady. More a feeling of excitement. This is all rather hard to believe."

The limo continued along the side of a huge wall with iron spikes on top of it.

"Almost there!" Lord Goodlad said.

As the limo rounded the corner, Bo saw a wide plaza in front of them with a beautiful fountain at its center, bedecked with magnificent statuary. The monument had a parklike setting on either side. Ahead was a long, tree-lined avenue, and as they continued around the curve, the majestic facade of Buckingham Palace came into view. At the center, atop the palace roof, the royal standard, Her Majesty's flag, fluttered in the breeze. Lady Goodlad murmured, "Well, at least we know she's home."

The chauffeur braked the limo to a halt in front of a large pair of gates

bearing golden coats of arms. He rolled down his window. A uniformed officer glanced inside the automobile and, recognizing Lord Goodlad, said, "Ah, milord! Just need to make a quick safety check. Bear with us!"

Panache sat up, curious to see what was going on, and Bo put her paws on the window ledge to obtain a better view. Several policemen surrounded the car, quickly and efficiently checking under the hood and in the trunk and sweeping a large gadget beneath the chassis.

Having made sure all was correct, the officer tapped the door. "Off you go, then!" He noticed Bo and added, "Is that the famous little cat?" Billy nodded. "She's a pretty creature! Have a good afternoon!" The officer saluted.

They drove through the iron gates, and as they approached an archway, Bo noticed two tall, navy-blue boxes with pointed roofs, one on either side. Each contained a sentry of the Queen's Guard, standing rigidly at attention, dressed in black trousers and a bright red jacket, with a high, furry hat on his head. The hats were so thick and bushy and shiny that Bo was reminded of her brother Tubs. It seemed very odd to wear a hat like a cat upon one's head.

A gentleman waved them on through the archway to an interior courtyard just beyond. A young lady carrying a clipboard was waiting for them on the steps of the main entrance.

As Lord Goodlad stepped out of the limousine, she said, "Welcome back, milord. We're very glad you're safe. Her Majesty is looking forward to seeing you."

"Thank you so much," Lord Goodlad responded. Turning to his wife, he said, "Time to put the cats in the carrier, Jessie. Billy, will you give her a hand?"

Bo was appalled as she and Panache were placed inside what seemed like a small duffel bag with mesh windows. She mewed in protest, but nobody paid any attention.

"Thomas will carry it," the lady with the clipboard said, waving to a fresh-faced young man who hurried down the steps.

The Goodlads and Billy followed the young lady through the Grand Entrance, with Thomas bringing up the rear, holding the cat carrier. They came to a spectacular staircase, lined with red carpet and flanked by an elaborately carved gold balustrade. High above its white and gold walls was a glass dome allowing sunlight to flood the hall. The staircase branched left and right, the two sides curving to meet at a landing that featured two tall, mirrored doors.

As they ascended, Billy admired the large royal portraits of Queen Elizabeth's ancestors lining the walls. There was so much to see that he felt he could barely take it all in—the ceramic urns, gold sconces and garlanding, majestic columns and stone statuary. He wished he could linger a moment, but they had reached the landing. Passing through the mirrored doors, they were ushered into an elegant green drawing room.

A distinguished-looking gentleman wearing a dark kilt, tasseled sporran, and smart black jacket with brass buttons stepped forward to greet them with a handshake.

"Good afternoon—Major Scotty Anderson, equerry to the queen. We're so glad to have you safely back with us, milord. And Lady Goodlad . . . always a pleasure. You've had quite an ordeal—I'm so sorry. This must be Mr. Bates . . . and, ah, the famous cats! An astonishing story—simply crackerjack! Koochy-coo, little one!" He waggled a finger at Bo through the mesh siding. "You can set the carrier on the settee by the window, Thomas.

Now"—he turned back to Billy—"just a few details of protocol. When you first meet Her Majesty, do not speak until spoken to. You will refer to her initially as 'Your Majesty,' and thereafter just 'ma'am'—as in 'jam.' Of course you'll be having tea, which will be somewhat informal, but obviously, wait until Her Majesty is seated before you seat yourself. When one leaves the royal presence, one takes care not to turn one's back on her until the last possible moment. So walk backward, facing her, until just before turning for the door. All clear?"

The lady with the clipboard popped her head around the door. "Her Majesty is ready, Major."

The equerry nodded. "Ah, good. Let's leave the kitties here with Thomas until Her Majesty asks for them. Follow me, please!"

As the Goodlads and Billy left the room with their escort, Bo's meows escalated to a wail. "Bill-eee!" she cried.

"*Bof!*" Panache grumbled. "All that fussing with our *coiffure* this morning—for what? I thought we would have an adventure! *En tout cas,* at least we are together, *n'est-ce pas, chérie*? And you smell divine!" He leaned against Bo affectionately.

"Honestly, Panache!" She cuffed him with her paw. "Ohh! There must be a way for us to get out of here." She stared intently at Thomas, who was sitting on a gilt chair, thumbing at a game on his cell phone. She mewed again, even more pitifully. Thomas looked up, and seeing that she had his attention, Bo redoubled her efforts.

The young man walked over to the carrier. Peering in through the mesh, he said, "What a sweet little thing you are. Are you feeling lonely?"

Bo gazed up at him, all innocence, her lovely violet eyes round as saucers. "Meow!" She tapped the mesh with a velvet paw.

"Okay, puss, come on out, then. . . ." Thomas unzipped the front of the cat carrier, but before he could so much as reach in to pick her up, Bo streaked past him and headed for the door, which was slightly ajar.

Thomas and Panache both blinked in surprise.

"*Attends, chérie!* Wait for me!" Panache took off after her.

"No! *Stop!*" Thomas yelled. But it was no use.

The cats tore down a long corridor lined with white settees and magnificent oil paintings. At the far end was yet another pair of mirrored doors. To the cats' surprise, the doors suddenly swung open to reveal four corgi dogs escorted by a lady-in-waiting. Bo and Panache skidded to a halt, the Oriental rug beneath them buckling like an accordion as they desperately fought for traction. Momentarily stunned, dogs and cats looked at each other for a good three seconds, and then . . . the chase was on.

Reversing course, Bo and Panache flew down the length of the corridor, the corgis in hot pursuit.

The lady-in-waiting cried out, "Monty! Holly! Linnet! Willow! *Heel!*" but to no avail.

The cats narrowly avoided Thomas, who came charging out of the green room only to collide with the lady-in-waiting. Disentangling themselves, the humans joined the chase. The animals had by now disappeared around a corner, and paying no attention to their surroundings, Bo and Panache raced down the grand staircase mere inches ahead of the panting corgis.

"This way, *chérie*!" Panache cried, and made a sharp left turn up a short flight of steps, across a marble hallway into a large room that featured a curved bank of windowed doors leading to the garden. One of the doors was slightly ajar. Emerging into the late-afternoon sun, the cats flew down a set of stone steps and streaked along a narrow path, past a couple of startled gardeners, and toward a cluster of trees, the corgis still close on their heels.

Thomas and the lady-in-waiting ran out onto the terrace and looked left and right. The gardeners pointed in the direction of the chase, and the pair took off once again.

Bo and Panache slid to a halt in front of a large oak tree. With one look at each other, they went straight up. As the cats scrambled higher and higher into the camouflage of the foliage, the corgis ran circles around the base of the tree, yapping and jumping. Then, satisfied that they had sent the intruders on their way, they trotted amiably back to

Thomas and the lady-in-waiting, who had come to a halt at a fork in the path.

"Blast! *Blast* it! What a bodge-up!" Thomas clasped his hair in frustration. "Now what do we do?"

The lady-in-waiting attempted to corral the happy corgis, who were puffed up and pleased with themselves. "Where on earth did they go?" she asked. "Oh, Monty! Stand *still!*"

Thomas scanned the gardens. "They could be on the other side of the lake by now," he said miserably.

Finally the lady-in-waiting said, "I suppose we'd better tell that nice young sailor . . . and Her Majesty, of course."

"She's going to be *so* cheesed off," Thomas groaned, and with a last desperate glance around, they turned and headed back toward the palace, the corgis padding contentedly behind them.

CHAPTER EIGHT

A Royal Adventure

HER MAJESTY QUEEN Elizabeth the Second, Sovereign of the Most Excellent Order of the British Empire, Head of the Commonwealth and Defender of the Faith, lifted the royal teapot.

"Shall I be 'mum'?" she asked sweetly, a glint of humor in her eye.

An attendant stepped forward and said, "Allow me, ma'am."

As tea was poured and finger sandwiches were served, Her Majesty continued. "It's really extraordinary what you accomplished, Mr. Bates. We are deeply indebted to you." She smiled at Lord Goodlad and added, "Barnaby is terribly important to the country . . . and to us. We happen to be rather fond of him."

Lord Goodlad bowed his head in acknowledgment. "Ever your humble servant, ma'am."

"And dear Jessie. What a nightmare. Are you still a little fragile?"

"Much better now that it's all over, ma'am, thank you."

"Yes, indeed. Well, I'm looking forward to meeting our phenomenal felines! They've quite eclipsed all other news these past weeks. Shall we send for them?"

There was a small tap at the door. Major Anderson opened it a crack. A brief conversation ensued, followed by a pause, and the major said wearily, "You'd better come in."

Thomas entered, looking rather ashen.

"What is it, Scotty?" Her Majesty inquired.

"Beg pardon, ma'am," the major said. "There's been a slight problem. Thomas here was in charge of the kitties. It seems they've disappeared."

Billy half rose out of his seat. "D-disappeared?" he stammered. Lady Goodlad put a hand to her chest.

The queen said, "Oh!"

"Tell us what happened, Thomas," Lord Goodlad said.

"The little one was crying, so I thought I would comfort her. I opened the carrier to take her out, and the next thing I knew, both cats had dashed into the hall. I went after them, of course, but unfortunately they met up with the corgis, ma'am, who chased them down the stairs and into the garden. I'm afraid we lost sight of them. . . ."

"Oh, those *naughty* doggies," Her Majesty said, sighing, with obvious affection. "We'd best put out an APW at once."

"Beg pardon, ma'am?" Billy inquired, his face flushed with embarrassment and anxiety.

"All-ports warning, old chap," Major Anderson explained. "Bit of an old-school expression—to stop offenders leaving the country and such. I'll get security on it right away, ma'am."

"You'd best go along, too, Billy," Lord Goodlad added. "Bo's likely to respond to your voice."

Observing protocol, Billy, Thomas, and Major Anderson backed hurriedly out of the room.

"What a nuisance!" the queen declared. "Thomas has a good heart, but he's new, and a trifle dim, I'm afraid. . . . How about another egg sandwich, Barnaby? Or would you prefer an éclair?"

In the oak tree, Bo sat wide-eyed and thoroughly shaken.

"I've always had such bad luck with dogs," she whimpered. "And there were *four* of them!"

"*Beh,* they were just playing," Panache said casually, and began washing his tail, which was still quite fluffed.

"All I wanted was to find Billy," Bo moaned dejectedly. "This was supposed to be our special day!"

"Well, we shall not find him up here," said Panache. "*Allons, ma petite.* We should go down."

"I'm *not* going back in there," Bo said, her voice rising in panic.

"Then let us go to those buildings over there," Panache suggested. "Someone will certainly recognize us. Remember, we are—how you say—*célèbres!*"

They padded cautiously along a curving path until they came to a wrought-iron lamppost and a large pair of wooden gates, which stood open. A quadrangle with the same pink earth as the Buckingham Palace courtyard was visible beyond, surrounded by a square of stately buildings with numerous arched windows and doors. Several cars were parked around the perimeter, and another cluster of oak trees stood in the center of the square. There was a pungent smell in the air. Panache raised his head and sniffed purposefully.

"*Des chevaux*," he said. "Horses."

A liveried gentleman crossed under the arch and entered one of the buildings.

"*Voilà!* We follow him!" said Panache purposefully. "Perhaps he can help us." Scampering after the gentleman, Bo meowed to get his

attention, but he was already striding across the polished brick floor, only to exit through another door on the far side, slamming it behind him.

Bo and Panache were stopped in their tracks by an astonishing sight. Standing before them were four gray horses, with immaculate red and gold trappings, and two uniformed riders. They were harnessed to a coach of such beauty that the cats were mesmerized. It appeared to be made entirely of gold, even the wheels. Ornately carved with lions, sea gods, fruits and vines, swords and plumes, the body of the coach also featured exquisitely painted panels. On the very top was a golden crown supported by three cherubs.

"*Incroyable!*" Panache murmured as he approached the extraordinary carriage.

"Watch out for the horses, Panache!" Bo called after him.

"Not to worry, *mon amie,* they are not real. Just part of the show, it seems. . . ."

Bo looked closely and realized Panache was right. Though detailed and lifelike, the horses and their riders were just life-size models.

The cats sniffed cautiously all around. Bo thought that the gilded and spoked carriage wheels seemed taller than Billy. The room the coach was housed in was spectacular, with vaulted ceilings and glass hurricane lamps suspended on slender chains.

"*Vraiment,*" Panache concluded. "Now *this* is what I call an adventure!"

"Not *now,* Panache . . . we *must* find someone to help us!" Bo said.

As they turned to head back out, the hair on Bo's back stood on end, for sitting in the entrance was another dog. She was quite small, and her wiry salt-and-pepper hair stuck out in all directions. She blinked and

peered at them with interest, her head tipped to one side.

As Bo prepared to flee, the dog said in a kindly voice, "Well, here's a rum do! Where'd you two spring from?"

Panache blinked. "*Excusez-moi?*" he asked.

Noticing Bo's hackles, the little dog continued. "What are ye so afeared of, lass? I've no wish to hurt ye. Haven't got but a few teeth left, and can't hear a thing besides, so ye'll have to speak up."

Panache looked at Bo. "What is she saying?"

Bo hesitated, keeping Panache between her and the odd little dog. "We're lost," she managed to croak.

"Yer *what?*"

"*Lost!*" Bo said as loudly as she could. "*We were supposed to meet with the queen. . . .*"

"Never!" The little dog looked interested.

"But FOUR DOGS chased us out of the palace!" Bo continued, gaining confidence.

"Chased, ye say?" The dog chuckled. "Not to worry, lass. Them four are full of jollies. Just puttin' on their parts, they are."

Panache was shaking his head. "I don't understand a word she is saying. . . ."

"I do," said Bo. "It's the way people speak where I was born." She summoned her courage and took a tentative step forward. "CAN YOU HELP? People will be looking for us. . . ."

The kindly old dog got up, stiff legged, wincing as she stretched. "Ye'd best follow me," she sighed. "Me master'll get yer out of this pickle."

CHAPTER NINE

Tea with Her Majesty

THE LITTLE DOG led the way into the big courtyard the cats had seen earlier.

"What is this place, *madame*?" Panache asked. "And what are you called?" But the dog obviously hadn't heard him, so he ran around to face her and repeated the question.

"Eh? I'm Molly. This here's the Royal Mews," she replied; then on Panache's blank look she added, "My heart, ye don't know much, do ye? This is where Her Majesty's horses live!"

As if on cue, a beautiful bay horse appeared, led by a groom.

"There y'are," Molly said. "That's Alderney. She's probably going out later today with that carriage there—the brougham. It takes the royal post and such back and forth."

"Do you know all the horses by name?" Bo asked.

"All thirty-four of 'em," Molly said proudly. "Been here a dog's age. Know every corner of this place, and every critter that comes through it. We've scores of coaches and carriages—cars, too—even a sleigh."

"Do you live in this mews?" Panache inquired.

"Course I do! In the gatehouse, with me master. He's the crown equerry—looks after this place. He'll be in the loose boxes about now. It's almost bedding-down time."

The cats ducked out of the way as another carriage and horse, with a liveried coachman at the reins, rattled past and out the main gates.

"In here," Molly indicated.

They entered a long bank of connected rooms. The walls were of pale green tile, and the immaculate floor was a geometric pattern of bricks, a thin sheen of water reflecting that it had just been hosed down. The rooms were divided into a series of wooden stalls, each with a nameplate signifying the occupant and his or her year of birth. Grooms quietly went about their business, attending to the feeding and comfort of several magnificent horses. There was a pungent smell of wood chips and hay, and the sound of contented munching, along with the occasional stomp of a hoof.

Molly nodded toward a beautiful bay who was being led into a loose box. "That there's Concorde—a young 'un. She'll have been in the riding school, getting used to harness. There's me master." She trotted over to a distinguished-looking gentleman who had one foot up on a bench as he held a cell phone to his ear.

"Righto, sir. I'll keep my eyes peeled," he was saying. He snapped the phone closed and looked down at Molly, who was pawing at his tweed trousers. "What is it, Molls? I know—it's almost time for supper."

The old dog trotted purposefully back to Bo and Panache and sat down next to them. The gentleman's eyes widened as he spotted the two cats.

"Good Lord, there they are! How on earth did you find them, old girl?" He flipped his phone open again, punched in a few numbers, and said, "Mission accomplished, sir! They've just wandered into the stables! Indeed I will. See you in a mo."

Bending down, he extended a hand and gently rubbed Bo under the chin. "Well, well. Fancy the famous cats showing up here. You've got the whole palace in a tizzy, you two!"

Molly wagged her tail with pleasure and rolled onto her back. The gentleman tickled her tummy. "Well done, old girl! Leave it to you to sniff out visitors!"

"What'd I tell yer?" Molly said to Bo and Panache, her gray eyes twinkling. "Someone'll be along to collect ye shortly . . . and I might just get me an extra biscuit tonight!"

Fifteen minutes later the cats were safely in the White Drawing Room of Buckingham Palace.

"That'll do, Thomas," Her Majesty was saying. "Tell Annie to bring the kitties a saucer of milk, and some fresh tea for us. And please shut the door after you." She turned back to Billy, who was holding Bo and Panache with a firm grip. "Now then, let's have a look at our intrepid explorers." She patted the seat next to her. "Come and sit by me."

With a glance at Lord Goodlad, who nodded reassuringly, Billy sat

gingerly on the end of the settee, next to the queen of England. Blushing slightly, he stammered, "Deepest apologies for the inconvenience, ma'am. . . ."

"Nonsense! It wasn't their fault, it was the dogs'—wasn't it, my dears? Not to worry, they won't be joining us for tea today." She stroked the cats with a sure hand that revealed her affinity for animals. "Aren't you both clever ones! What did you think of my stables, then? Did you see my lovely horses?"

There was another tap at the door, and Major Anderson reappeared. "The prime minister, ma'am," he announced.

"Ah, Duncan! You made it!" the queen said, as a robust-looking gentleman with a thick crop of sandy hair entered the room. He was holding a

leather carrier much like the one Bo and Panache had escaped from. "And you brought His Lordship. What fun! Barnaby, you know Duncan White, but I don't think you've met his most trusted friend—the only member of our cabinet to be utterly discreet."

The head of Her Majesty's government placed the carrier on the floor.

"Your Majesty." He bowed, then turned to the Goodlads. "Barney, Jessie—sorry to hear of your ordeal. It's good to see you both. Her Majesty mentioned that she'd be receiving you and the honored cats, and she invited me to come along. We felt Walpole should pay his respects as well." He unzipped the carrying case. "Out you come, then, laddie!"

An elegant gray cat emerged, his tail held high. Lord Goodlad hooted with laughter. On the settee, Bo and Panache sat up with interest.

Her Majesty smiled. "Forgive our frivolity! I just couldn't resist bringing my feline-loving friends together. . . ."

Bo felt a familiar prickle on the back of her neck, and suddenly her heart thumped with excitement. She jumped down off the couch and ran to touch noses with the newcomer.

"Maximillian?" she cried.

"Boadicea! I *knew* it was you!" the other cat cried delightedly. "I saw the newspapers and I've been bursting with pride ever since!"

As Panache joined them, Lady Goodlad remarked, "Look! How adorable, Duncan! They've made friends already!"

"Panache! This is my brother Maximillian!" Bo explained breathlessly.

"*Monsieur*." Panache greeted Maximillian with a respectful nod of his head. He looked at Bo. "*Incroyable, chérie!* Your family continues to surprise, *non*?"

"But fancy meeting you *here*!" Bo was beside herself with joy. "I've been searching for you forever! How on earth do you happen to be with the prime minister?"

As fresh tea was served and the queen asked Billy to share details of the rescue, Maximillian told his story to Bo and Panache.

"That day long ago, when we all escaped from the bicycle basket—the day I was sure that Withers, the dreadful butler, was intending to throw us in the river and I said we must all run in different directions? Well, I

ran and ran, and eventually I made my way to a hotel in a nearby village—"

"So did I!" Bo interrupted him. "But there was a horrible dog at the back door!"

"Well, I went in the front," Maximillian continued. "I spotted two gentlemen having lunch in the restaurant and made my presence known to them during the cheese course. Upon seeing my bedraggled condition, one of the gentlemen took pity on me, and the next thing I knew, I was traveling back to London with him on the train. A very decent chap—turns out he was the minister of education, who had been having lunch with the chancellor of the local university. To cut a long story short, the prime minister had recently lost his Lilac Scottish Fold—a beloved cat by the name of Woolsack. I was offered as a replacement, and I've been at Number Ten Downing Street ever since."

Panache looked impressed.

"You always were the cleverest in the family," Bo marveled.

"But what about you, Bo? How did you come to be the warrior queen of the high seas?"

Before Bo could reply, there was yet another knock at the door. Major Scotty Anderson came into the drawing room once again, this time looking rather harried.

"Beg pardon, ma'am. The lady in question has arrived." Dropping his voice, he whispered, "And might I say, she *is* as effusive as her correspondence suggested."

The queen blinked. "Ah, yes! Well, she's very prompt. Dear Goodlads, Duncan . . . we felt obliged to allow our next guest a brief audience. She's been extremely adamant that she has something of relevance to contribute to our gathering this afternoon. Show her in, Scotty."

Teacups raised, the assembled guests turned to face the door. Major Scotty Anderson took a deep breath. Lifting his gaze to the ornately decorated ceiling, he intoned, "Mrs. Edith Edge, ma'am."

CHAPTER TEN

The Surprise Guest

AN IMPOSING FIGURE swept into the drawing room. Almost as wide as she was tall, she was swathed in taffeta that rustled as she walked. Pearls and spectacles on a chain bounced about her neck, and her hair was piled high atop her jowled face. Thomas, burdened with two new carrying cases, followed behind—stumbling every now and then as the buxom lady bowed, bobbed, and curtseyed her way toward the queen. Billy and the prime minister scooped up their respective cats to keep them out of harm's way.

"Mrs. Edge, good afternoon." The queen extended her hand. "May I present Lord and Lady Goodlad, Prime Minister White, and—"

Breathless, Mrs. Edge sank to one knee and grasped the royal hand, pumping it vigorously.

"Oh, *such* a pleasure, Your Majesty! *So* kind of you! As I believe I mentioned, I'm a member of the GCCF—that's the Governing Council of the Cat Fancy," she explained, with a nod to the prime minister. "I'm not sure you're aware, ma'am, that I was recently elevated to chairperson of the Eastern Counties Cat-Lovers Association. My specialty, of course, is

Persians. . . ." Momentarily distracted by the tea cakes, which were inches from her nose, she added, "Ooh! Are those éclairs?"

Extricating her hand from Mrs. Edge's, the queen dexterously swept up the plate and offered her a pastry.

Mrs. Edge took the largest one and popped it into her mouth. *"Delicious!"* she gushed, dabbing an errant splotch of cream with her pinky finger.

With what sounded like a suppressed sneeze, Lord Goodlad reached for the biscuit plate. "I believe I'll have another one of these!" He winked as he proffered it to the other guests. "Billy, Duncan?"

Mrs. Edge brushed the crumbs from her ample chest. "*Now!* The reason I was so anxious to see you!" She donned her spectacles and peered at Bo, who had begun to shiver in Billy's arms. "*There's* the little minx that's been causing all the commotion! Of course, I recognized her instantly! I never forget a face! And *you* must be the sailor boy. . . ."

Billy looked bewildered. "But I don't believe we've met, ma'am?"

"Well, of course not. That cat began her life with me, *long* before she met you. I'm her breeder!" Mrs. Edge gave Thomas a sharp nudge. The young man had been standing as if rooted to the floor, still holding the two carriers. With a start, he set them down, and like a magician performing a grand finale, Mrs. Edge unzipped one of the bags with a flourish. "I am proud to present the mother of Little Bo—Champion Sarabande, Reina de Barcelona, Pasión y la Danza."

She lovingly lifted up a magnificent white Persian cat and held her high for all to see.

Lady Goodlad clapped her hands and murmured, "Oh my—she's lovely!"

"Yes. You can imagine how I simply couldn't resist showing off a little." Mrs. Edge set the cat down. "The moment I saw the photographs in the press, and read the royal calendar, I just *knew* Your Majesty would wish to—" But that was as far as she got.

Bo had squirmed out of Billy's arms, and now she jumped down and raced across the carpet to touch noses with the beautiful white Persian. She was joined a mere second later by Maximillian.

Prime Minister White exclaimed, "Good Lord!"

"There! You see? You *see*? They know each other!" Mrs. Edge cried triumphantly.

The queen began, "It would certainly appear so. . . ." Her attention turned to the second cat carrier on the floor, from which emanated a low feline growl. "And shall we surmise that you've brought the sire, as well?" she asked drily.

"Oh. *Him*." Mrs. Edge unzipped the second bag, and a magnificent black cat stepped out. "They're inseparable, I'm afraid. His name is Bounder. Unfortunately Sarabande will not go *anywhere* without him."

Bo was suffused with joy. "Mama—and, oh, Papa!" she kept crying,

alternately mewing and purring. She and Maximillian pressed themselves lovingly against the two beautiful newcomers, who seemed equally delighted to see them.

Sarabande was saying, "My dears! My *dears* . . . how wonderful! I never dared hope that I would see you again." She nuzzled them tenderly.

Bounder murmured, "This is grand, just grand—isn't it Sara? *So,* little Boadicea . . . you *did* survive that terrible day in the snow. And Maximillian—I knew you'd outsmart any villains who crossed *your* path. But tell us all—right from the beginning!"

As Mrs. Edge prattled on about everything to do with her cats, their breeding, and her forthcoming Eastern Counties cat show, Bo introduced Panache to her parents. All five cats huddled on the carpet together as she and Maximillian told of their many adventures.

"Oh, and Mama—I saw Tubs in Paris! And he is *so* happy! He belongs to a famous chef, Monsieur Pelouche. And in Italy I found Samson, who was performing in a circus with lions and tigers—and he jumps through fire with the biggest lion every night!"

Panache said, "Tell them about Polly, *chérie*. . . ."

Bo continued, describing their confrontation with the feral cats in the Colosseum in Rome, and how Panache had defended her and they had discovered Polly. "And Papa, she was very ill! But now she lives there safely in the British ambassador's home."

Maximillian's ears twitched, "Does she, by Jove? I must remember that!" He took up his part of the story, describing his fortunate introduction to the prime minister and how busy and fascinating life was for both of them.

Bounder said, "And you, Bo, and Panache here, did a brave and marvelous thing—rescuing the Goodlads when they were in such peril. The news is everywhere on the grapevine. I am *so* proud of you both. You're a credit to our species." He gazed into his daughter's beautiful violet eyes. "You've certainly proved worthy of your name, little Boadicea." Glancing

at Billy, he added, "Your Mr. Bates seems to be a fine young man. I foresee good things ahead for him. And Panache—splendid fellow! Thank you for befriending my little girl. I can only hope you'll continue to enjoy each other's company as much as Sara and I do."

Panache dipped his head with respect. "*Merci, monsieur.* That is my wish also."

Bo asked, "What of Princess, Mama? Is she still at home?"

Sarabande smiled. "Yes. Despite your father's best attempts, she continues to be a fireside cat. Very beautiful, of course. A trifle spoiled."

Bounder added, "She should have been with us today, but we will relay your news to her . . . and we will all meet again one day, I am certain of it."

Bo could hardly bring herself to ask, "And Mr. Withers? That horrible man, who wanted to put us in the river . . . is he still at the house?"

Sarabande shook her head. "He's gone. My lady discovered through the people at the pet shop, and also the vet, that he had never fulfilled her wishes concerning you kittens. He went the next day."

Mrs. Edge had paused for breath and another éclair.

Looking somewhat dazed, Her Majesty seized the opportunity and discreetly rang for Major Anderson. She sighed and stood up. "I'm afraid it is time to bid you all farewell. I have to spend a while with the diplomatic boxes before the grandchildren arrive."

"Ah, yes! Duty calls, I understand." Mrs. Edge scooped up Sarabande and placed her in the cat carrier. Batting her eyes at Major Anderson, she pleaded, "Would you help me with the black cat, Major? He is rather heavy! By the way, I do *so* admire your splendid kilt! It's Anderson clan, am I right?" She continued to chat on, even while being ushered out of the room. "Good-bye, all!" She waved. "*Such* a pleasure! Remember, ma'am, April the seventh, King's Lynn, for the cat show, if you have a *moment* to stop by. . . ." The door closed softly behind her.

Bo sat down. Then, unable to contain her joy, she leaped up, spun several circles, then sat down again.

"Wasn't that extraordinary!" She purred. "Oh, Panache! Isn't the palace beautiful? Isn't Her Majesty lovely? Isn't London wonderful? Isn't life *amazing*!"

Panache smiled at her fondly and said to Maximillian, "A pity she is so *réservée, non?*"

Her Majesty said, "This has been a splendid afternoon, *great* fun. Oh! I almost forgot. One last treat! Now where did I put it? Ah, yes. Barnaby—would you pass me that little box on the side table there?" She turned to Billy. "Now, Mr. Bates. In recognition of your courage and selflessness in protecting the lives of others, it is our pleasure to award you the Queen's Commendation for Bravery."

She opened the small leather case and removed a delicate silver badge resembling a spray of laurel leaves. Pinning it to his jacket, she murmured kindly, "We are deeply grateful."

Major Anderson came back into the room. "Excuse me, Your Majesty. The press office was asking if a quick photo might be in order. The tabloids are extremely persistent, I'm afraid."

"Of course."

A photographer who had obviously been hovering just outside the door came in, several cameras dangling about his neck. The queen of England positioned herself beside the Goodlads and the prime minister, who was holding Maximillian. As Billy swept Bo and Panache into his arms and joined them, the camera shutters clicked in rapid succession, and flashbulbs temporarily dazzled them, thus capturing the happy moment forever.

CHAPTER ELEVEN

A Party and Proposals

DRIVING BACK TO the yacht, Billy was at a loss for words. As the wondrous events of the afternoon played over and over in his mind, he sat with Bo on his lap, a bemused smile on his face.

Lord Goodlad chuckled. "Well, that was extremely entertaining!" He indicated Billy's medal. "I don't even have one of those, old chap!"

Lady Goodlad patted Billy's hand comfortingly. "Dear Billy. What a lovely turn of events. We are so fortunate to have you in our lives."

"Speaking of which," Lord Goodlad interjected, "I think you're aware, Billy, that Captain Ian is intending to retire within a couple of months. Naturally, we'd love to have you take his place. Interested?"

Billy gasped. "Oh, sir—it would be my great honor."

"Splendid!"

As they approached Tower Bridge, they spotted *Legend* at her mooring. She was decked with fairy lights from the tips of her tall masts to the ends of her bow and stern.

"That's Wally's doing, I'll be bound!" Lord Goodlad smiled.

"Oh—and there's more press. I don't know about you two, but I'm ready for a glass of champagne!"

It was a merry party aboard the yacht that night. Marie-Claire and Lucy were enthralled to hear the details of the royal visit. When they heard about the corgi chase and how Bo and Panache had disappeared, Marie-Claire scooped Bo into her arms and hugged her close. "Always *aventureuse*, eh, leetle one?"

Lucy plied Lady Goodlad for details of the palace, the royal china, and the quality of the finger sandwiches.

Wally thumped Billy on the back and admired his medal. "That's a bit of all right, isn't it? Do I have to call you 'sir' now?"

Billy punched him playfully. "I'll settle for 'mate'!" He grinned.

Captain Ian, presiding over all, wandered about, hands clasped behind his back, nodding and beaming at everyone. "This'll be a memorable entry in the ship's log," he confided to Lord Goodlad.

After a splendid supper, the Goodlads retired to their cabin, and Billy and Marie-Claire wandered out on the forward deck beneath the twinkling fairy lights and the stars above. They gazed at the Tower Bridge, now magnificently illuminated, and the skyline of London beyond. Billy placed an arm about Marie-Claire's waist, and she nestled her head on his shoulder. He quietly told her of Lord Goodlad's offer to have him take command of the yacht when Captain Ian retired.

"Oh, Billee! How *merveilleux!*" Marie-Claire's eyes sparkled with delight. "I am so proud!"

Billy gazed at her with adoration. "His will be hard shoes to fill," he murmured. "But now we can make plans for our future together. May I ask Captain Ian to marry us once we're back in the south of France?"

She replied without hesitation, "I would like that very much."

Above them, on the roof of the wheelhouse, Bo and Panache sat quietly, each reflecting on the extraordinary events of the day. Sighing contentedly, Panache said, "I think that was the best adventure we *ever* had."

"Mmmm." Bo nodded dreamily.

Noticing Marie-Claire and Billy below them, Panache said,

"They're a bit like us, *non?*"

"What do you mean?" Bo asked.

"Well, *you* know. . . ."

Bo looked at him and blinked. "No. I don't."

"Oh—er—well, like Lord and Lady Goodlad, or your lovely mama and papa—"

"They liked you! I could tell," Bo interrupted him.

"—or like my great-great-great-grandfather Moustafa and his sixth wife," Panache continued, pressing his point. "Oh, phooey! Look, are you my friend or aren't you?"

"Of course I am!"

"Really?" He brightened. "My best friend, forever?"

"Yes."

"That's all right, then."

"I'm afraid I don't understand . . . ," Bo teased, for she understood perfectly. "Is that what you're trying to say? That we're each other's best friend?"

He shook his head. Touching the tip of her nose, he replied, "More than that, *chérie*."

Bo studied him, her heart bursting with affection. "You know, Panache, you're very dashing in that silly collar."

He raised his chin an inch. "But of course!" he replied. Then, with a sideways glance at her, he smiled and said simply, "I think I could get used to it."

PANACHE
BO

Little Bo, a tiny gray cat with a big name—
Bonnie Boadicea—lives a life of big adventure.
Join in her journey with

Little Bo,
Little Bo in France, and
Little Bo in Italy

Other books by Julie Andrews Edwards
& Emma Walton Hamilton

Thanks to You: Wisdom from Mother & Child
The Great American Mousical
Simeon's Gift
Dragon: Hound of Honor

and the Dumpy the Dumptruck books:

Dumpy and the Firefighters
Dumpy to the Rescue!
Dumpy's Apple Shop
Dumpy's Extra-Busy Day
Dumpy's Happy Holiday
Dumpy's Valentine